D1604786

JUSTICE LEAGUE

STORM SURGE

By **Donald Lemke**

Illustrated by
Patrick Spaziante

HARPER FESTIVAL
An Imprint of HarperCollins Publishers

HarperFestival is an imprint of HarperCollins Publishers.

Justice League: Storm Surge
Copyright © 2017 DC Comics.
JUSTICE LEAGUE and all related characters and elements © & ™ DC Comics.
(s17)

HARP37203
Manufactured in China.
Library of Congress Control Number: 2016952955
ISBN 978-0-06-236079-3

Book design by Erica De Chavez
17 18 19 20 21 SCP 10 9 8 7 6 5 4 3 2 1
❖
First Edition

THE HEROES AND VILLAINS IN THIS BOOK!

AQUAMAN

Aquaman lives in the underwater city of Atlantis. As King of the Seven Seas, he communicates with sea creatures and protects them with his trident spear.

SUPERMAN

Superman, also known as the Man of Steel, has many amazing superpowers. To hide his super hero identity, he works as reporter Clark Kent at the *Daily Planet* newspaper.

WONDER WOMAN

Diana Prince is an Amazon Princess from the island of Themyscira. As Wonder Woman, she fights for peace and justice, wielding her Lasso of Truth.

THE FLASH

The Flash is also known as the Fastest Man Alive. With incredible speed, the lightning-quick super hero wastes no time taking down the world's worst villains.

BLACK MANTA

Black Manta's high-tech uniform allows him to breathe underwater. The super-villain builds weapons and gadgets to gain control of the ocean and its creatures.

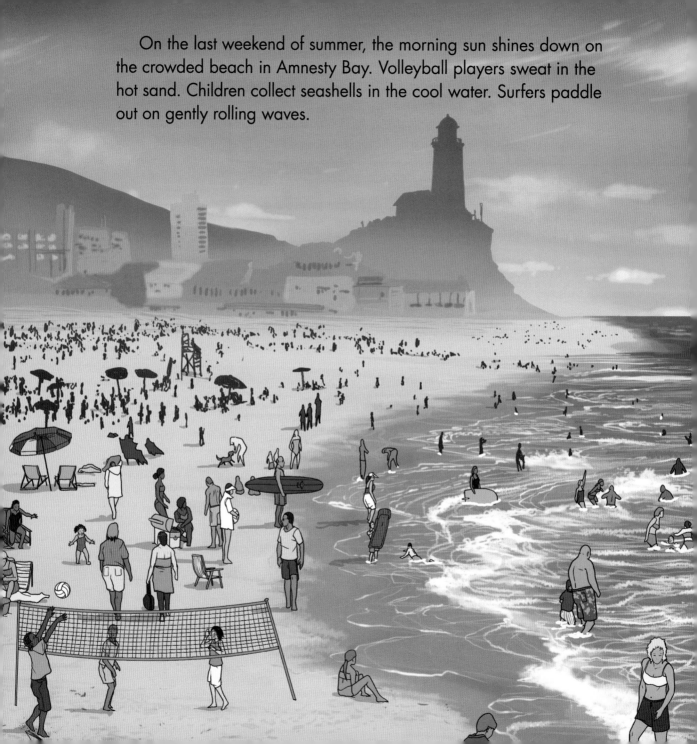

On the last weekend of summer, the morning sun shines down on the crowded beach in Amnesty Bay. Volleyball players sweat in the hot sand. Children collect seashells in the cool water. Surfers paddle out on gently rolling waves.

From her chair, a lifeguard spots a large swell on the horizon. It quickly grows bigger and bigger and bigger. *Breep!* She blows her whistle and raises a red warning flag.

"Tidal wave!" she cries to the crowd below.

Parents grab their children and flee toward nearby cars.

Surfers paddle rapidly toward shore, but one can't escape the rushing wave. *Smash!* It crashes over him.

The lifeguard grabs her safety buoy. Before she reaches the water—*fwoosh!*—
the young surfer bursts from the ocean like a dolphin. He has been rescued by
the King of the Seven Seas . . . Aquaman!

The super hero carries the surfer to shore and then glances back at the bay. Swimmers struggle in the deadly surf. Bobbing ships fire emergency flares. A thick wall of clouds rises behind them like flames. Aquaman watches carefully, looking for a clue in the chaos.

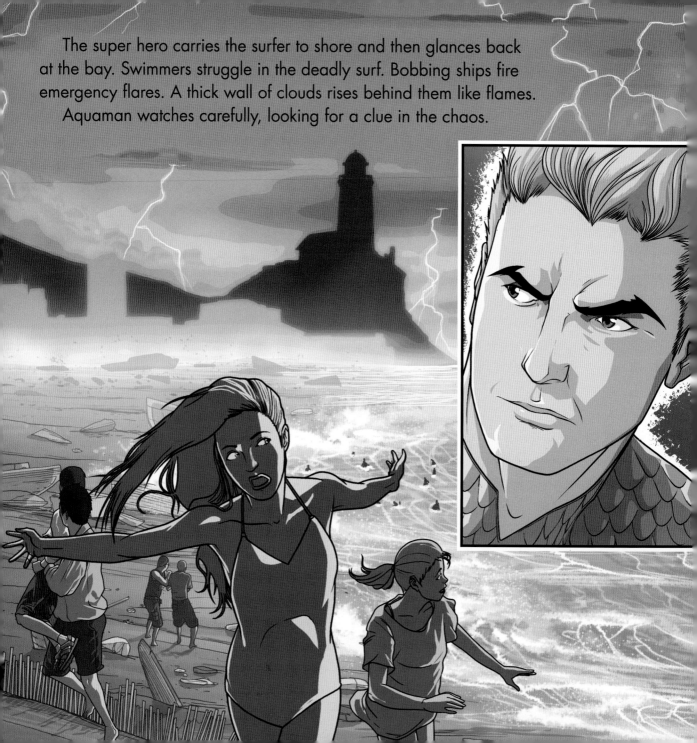

Finally he calls the other members of the Justice League. Superman and Wonder Woman soon appear out of the red clouds above.

A split second later, a red-and-yellow streak rockets across the surface of the bay. "Looks like I've found my sea legs," The Flash jokes as he arrives on shore.

With his super-hearing, Superman notices the distant rumbling of another storm surge. "Get everyone ashore!" he tells the heroes. "I'll keep this wave at bay."

Aquaman dives underwater and guides swimmers to the surface where Wonder Woman rescues them with her Lasso of Truth. The Flash speedily carries beachgoers to higher ground.

Meanwhile, Superman fills his powerful lungs with air.
The air quickly cools inside them. *Fwoosh!* The Man of Steel
blasts the oncoming wave with his Freeze Breath.

Superman freezes wave after monster wave. "We need to locate the eye of this hurricane," he says between breaths.

"And fast!" adds The Flash from shore.

Aquaman surfaces. "I already have," he reports. "Two red eyes, to be exact."

As The Flash guards the beach, Aquaman leads the other heroes underwater. On the seafloor stands a high-tech machine. A giant propeller spins atop the machine, swirling the surrounding water like a whirlpool.

Then Aquaman spots the glowing, evil eyes of his worst enemy. "Black Manta!" he shouts.

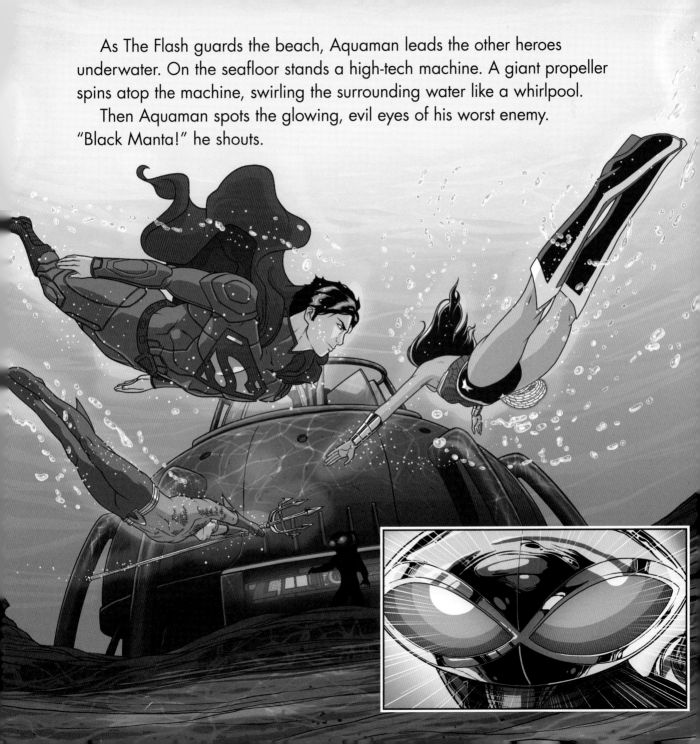

"What are you doing, Manta?" Wonder Woman demands.

"Isn't it obvious?" the villain replies. "I'm taking the world by storm!"

Black Manta turns a dial on the machine. The giant propeller rotates faster and faster. An underwater tornado swirls upward and fuels the hurricane above.

Superman laughs. "That's funny," he begins, "because the forecast calls for a heat wave!"

The Man of Steel's eyes glow red. He aims his heat vision at the machine.

"Wait!" Aquaman cries out. "You'll turn this entire bay into a giant steam pot." He points at turtles, jellyfish, and other sea creatures nearby.

Black Manta turns up the dial again, and his storm machine reaches full strength.

"If we don't do something, we're in for an awfully long night," Wonder Woman urges the others.

Her words give Aquaman an idea.

After a quick plan, the Man of Steel swims toward the ocean's surface.
"What's the matter?" asks Black Manta. "Does he have bigger fish to fry?"
The villain lets out a deep laugh.
As he does, Aquaman ties Wonder Woman's lasso to his trident.

"Nope," Aquaman says. "We like to practice catch and release."
Aquaman hurls his trident toward the seafloor. Wonder Woman's lasso
unravels behind it. *Clank!* The spear hooks the metal machine.

Wonder Woman grasps the other end of her golden lasso. She pulls the storm machine from the seafloor and speeds toward the surface. "No!" Black Manta cries. He grabs on to his rising machine.

Wonder Woman soars out of the water. Black Manta
and his machine dangle from her lasso like fish on a hook.
With a twist of her lasso, Wonder Woman unhooks the
trident and flings the machine and Black Manta into the air.

Nearby, Superman's eyes glow red again. This time, his heat vision reaches its target. *Ka-blam!* The machine explodes in midair, and the blast sends Black Manta tumbling back to the sea and into Aquaman's waiting hands.

Onshore, The Flash twirls his arms like a twin-engine plane. He fans the burning pieces that have landed on the beach so the flames die down.

Moments later, Aquaman drags Black Manta onto the beach.
The other Justice League members and several officers await them.
"Nice catch!" Wonder Woman tells Aquaman.
"You know," he replies, handing the villain over to the police,
"I think this one's a keeper."